Old MacDonald Had a Dragon

By
Ken
Baker

Illustrated by
Christopher
Santoro

Amazon Children's Publishing

"**Old MacDonald had a farm, E-I-E-I-O.**
And on that farm he had a dragon, E-I-E-I—"

"Not so fast," mooed the cow as it moseyed up to the farmhouse. "I've got a beef with you."

"Dragons don't belong on farms," the cow said.

"It's my farm," said Old MacDonald. "I can have a dragon if I want one."

"Either the dragon moves out, or this moo moves on," mooed the cow.

Faster than the farmer could sing E-I-E-I-O, the dragon swooped out of the sky, gulped down the cow, and swallowed it whole.

"Delightful dairy," said the dragon. With a lick of its lips and a flash of fire, it whipped its wings and flew away.

The farmer frowned. "Too bad," he said. "I'll miss that cow, even if it was a bit bull-headed."

"Old MacDonald had a farm, E-I-E-I-O. And on that farm he had a pig, E-I-E-I-O. With an oink, oink here and an—"

"Wait one mud-stinkin' minute," oinked the pig. "As long as there's a dragon on this farm, there'll be no more 'oink, oink here' or 'oink, oink there.'

Adios. This hog is hitting the road."

Faster than the farmer could sing E-I-E-I-O, the dragon swooped out of the sky, gulped down the pig, and swallowed it whole.

"Savory swine," said the dragon. With a lick of its lips and a flash of fire, it flapped its wings and flew away—kind of.

The farmer wrinkled his nose and frowned. "Good riddance. That stinky sow always smelled of trouble. Besides, I really like my dragon."

"Old MacDonald had a farm, E-I-E-I-O.
And on that farm he had a sheep—"

A ram charged up the steps and butted Old MacDonald right out of his chair.

"You can't pull the wool over our eyes," baaed the old ram. "You get rid of that dragon, or you can kiss your wool socks good-bye."

Faster than the farmer could sing E-I-E-I-O, the dragon flopped out of the sky, gulped down the ram and the whole farmyard of sheep, and swallowed them whole.

"Marvelous mutton," said the dragon.
With a lick of its lips and a flash of fire,
it wilted its wings and waddled away.

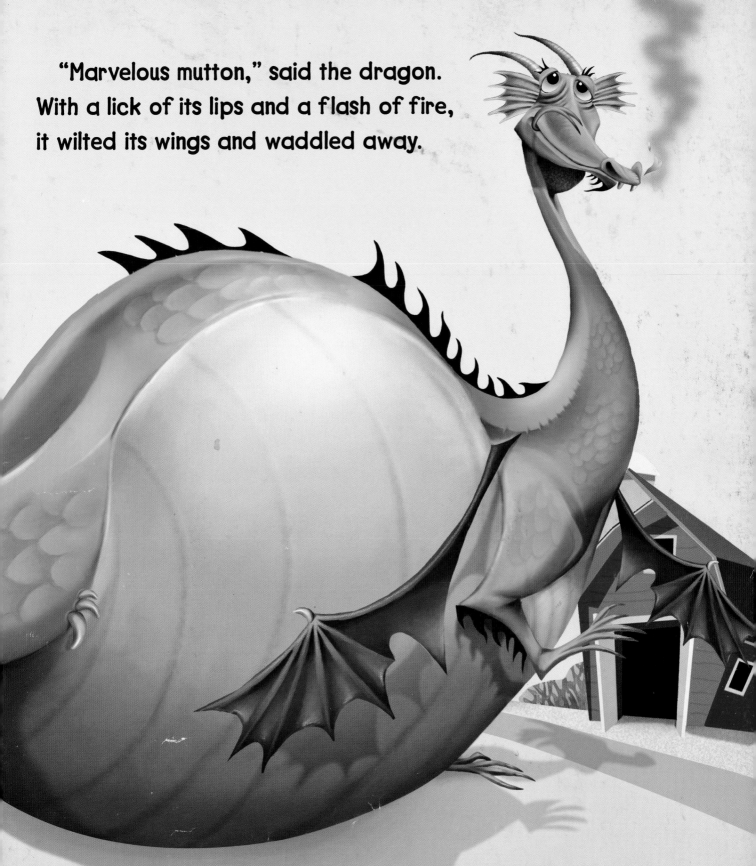

The farmer folded his arms across his chest and frowned.
"I'm not so sure that dragon is a good idea after all," he said.
"I might need those sheep and their woolly socks to keep my
feet warm at night."

"Old MacDonald had a farm, E-I-E-I-O.
And on that farm he had a dog—"

"Keep me out of your two-bit tune," barked the dog. "I saw what happened to the cow. I saw what happened to the pig. And I saw what happened to the sheep. I don't want to be dragon feed."

Faster than the farmer could sing E-I-E-I-O, the dragon dragged itself across the yard, gulped down the dog, and swallowed it whole.

"Delectable doggy," said the dragon. With a lick of its lips and a flash of fire, it folded its wings, flopped down, and fell asleep.

The farmer jumped off the porch and stormed across the yard.

"Now wait one doggone minute," he said, kicking the
dragon in the snout. "Give me back my Roscoe."

Faster than the farmer could sing E-I-E-I-O, the dragon stood, gulped down the farmer, and swallowed him whole.

Inside the dragon, the farmer
scratched his head and smiled.

"Old MacDonald had a dragon, E-I-E-I-O. And in that dragon he had a cow, a pig, a ram, some sheep, and a dog. E-I-E-I-O.

With a moo-oink-baa-woof here, and a moo-oink-baa-woof there. Here a moo-oink-baa-woof—"

The farmer and all the animals shot out of the dragon's mouth and tumbled onto the ground in a slimy heap.

"Terrible tummy ache," howled the dragon.

With a frown on its lips and one
last belch of fire, it whipped its
wings and flew up and away—
for good.

The farmer smiled, plucked his guitar, and sang, "Old MacDonald had a farm, E-I-E-I-O. And on that farm he had a—"

To Karissa, Spencer, Alisa, Austin, and Ashlyn—
for all the joy and inspiration you give me
—K. B.

For Anna and Alex
—C. S.

Amazon Publishing
Attn: Amazon Children's Books
P.O. Box 400818
Las Vegas, NV 89149
www.amazon.com/amazonchildrenspublishing

Library of Congress Cataloging-in-Publication Data
Baker, Ken, 1962-
Old MacDonald had a dragon / by Ken Baker ; illustrated by Christopher
Santoro. — 1st ed.
p. cm.
Summary: The new dragon on Old MacDonald's farm puts all the other
animals, and the farmer, in peril.
ISBN 978-0-7614-6175-3 (hardcover) — ISBN 978-0-7614-6243-9 (ebook)
[1. Dragons—Fiction. 2. Domestic animals—Fiction. 3. Animal
sounds—Fiction. 4. Farms—Fiction.] I. Santoro, Christopher, ill. II.
Title.
PZ7.B17428Old 2012
[E]—dc23
2011036607

The illustrations are rendered digitally.
Book design by Anahid Hamparian
Editor: Marilyn Brigham

Printed in Malaysia (M)
First edition
10 9 8 7 6 5 4 3 2 1